Milton
and the
Morning Monk

By Robert B. McDiarmid

For Rick Murray

Love is our true destiny. We do not find the meaning of life
by ourselves alone - we find it with another.
- Thomas Merton

So many beautiful friends helped bring this work to life

Stained Glass Illustrations by Karen Bauermeister
Hand Drawn Sketches by Mike Blassingham
The Letters written by Gary Akenhead & Calvin MacLean
Photography by Wanda Lotus

The prairie fog danced across the moon that showed through my window. I had moved my bed up against the window just for late nights like this.

I never slept well, and would find myself staring out, finding comfort in the silence and watching the stars churn by in the heavens. Many early mornings would find me listening for them, the winter moon illuminating my face.

Far in the distance I could hear the immortal bellow of a freight train whistle and its chattering down the tracks. Right on schedule, the early bell rang from the monastery. I imagined bleary-eyed monks shuffling their way to morning prayers. I spent my childhood in the shadow of it.

The monastery stood on the bluff above my small Idaho town. Bell tolls and the siren sound of Gregorian chant would get caught on the wind.

They would sing the Ubi caritas.

Ubi caritas et amor, Deus ibi est.
Where charity and love are, there God is.

I can remember humming along with it. I still keep a binder of all sorts of musical arrangements of the simple text. The Gregorian melody was composed sometime between the fourth and tenth centuries, though some scholars believe the text dates from early Christian gatherings before the formalization of the Mass.

The text is inspired and translated from Corinthians 13. Saint Paul says you can have all these gifts, all these amazing ideas, but if you don't have love - then you have nothing. Paul says, "If I give all I possess to the poor and give over my body to hardship that I may boast, but do not have love, I gain nothing."

I was a gangling teenager ginger, sort of a nerdy Ron Howard. Nothing seemed to fit, literally or figuratively. So I retreated into my books and my romantic notions of love. I would fall in love with everything in my path, from the family dog to characters in teenage fictions to school friends. It caused a fair amount of heartbreak in my young life - as many people didn't seem to find the value in love as I did. It became a passion of mine to find the love in everything, and sometimes that made me blind to other motives and other intents.

Moscow, Idaho - 1975

"You need to protect yourself, Bill," Pop would say to me one day on a walk into town. "You can't just love so completely, so blindly."

"But isn't that what they tell us in church? Love others as you'd have them love you? Love is unconditional!" I naively protested.

"Humans have never really figured that one out, sport. Love, unfortunately, comes with all kinds of conditions. Unqualified love is not a human quality. I think when the Bible describes unconditional love, they are talking about God."

"I get so confused."

"We all do, bud. At your age there are so many answers you want, and they simply don't always come easy. Be gentle on yourself. Don't push so hard. Let's see what adventures come your way - by simply being available for them."

"I guess so," I said with a soft sigh.

"It'll happen. Your mom and I knew we were for one another the very first time we met. It was the most romantic thing, so much so that it hurt, and you just can't fake or make something like that happen."

Particularly when it came to learning how romance worked - I was a total failure. I was an awkward boy who fell and stumbled into adolescence. I seemed to have none of the tools that other teenage boys had naturally. I was good at sports, but not great. I was so nervous talking to girls that they avoided me. It was a small town so people coupled up quickly. I entered my senior year feeling like everyone around me was moving on to what was next in life and leaving me behind.

I think it felt like a puzzle-piece clicking into place when in the fall of 1976 I left for seminary. My father was very pleased that all my introspection and seemingly disorganized youth had actually turned into something. When I announced my intentions, for him it all suddenly made perfect sense. His son would become a monk.

Mom didn't understand. I would catch her looking at me that final summer. She mourned it, with reflections of grandchildren laughing and frolicking, the life she'd imagined for me, falling away in tears like ghosts in the corners of her eyes.

September 1977 - St. Gertrude's Seminary

The fall colors of the Willamette Valley were simply on fire, the ornate orange stone buildings disappearing in the sea of leaves and green grasses. I walked into my residence hall. Etched in the stone above the door, "The Hope of the Harvest is in the Seed." I was so optimistic, so convinced.

The strict schedule really appealed to me, the devotional routine. I would arise in the dark, and take a deep breath, and thank God. I would sneak down to the gym to work out. I'd always be showered and in perfect robes when everyone else showed up for breakfast before morning prayers. It earned me the moniker "Morning Monk" from the not-quite-awake brothers coming into the hall with a weary nod. I would walk to the chapel and ring the morning bell, calling everyone to the first shared prayers of the day.

One morning after prayers, I was stopped by the Abbot.

"Good morning, Mr Emory."

"Father," I said, politely greeting him.

"I was wondering if we could ask a favor of you. We have a student who came here from Quebec, eastern Canada, and his English skills are not as good as they need to be. I'm afraid he has withdrawn a bit, and I am wondering if you might tutor him? You listed French as a language you learned in your studies?"

"Yes, Father, but classroom French. I ... I'm not sure if I could converse."

"But you could help a fellow seminarian to find his roots? I really think once he gets some confidence, he'll be a great asset to us here."

"I am here to serve, Father. I'd be glad to meet him and help in way I can."

"Good, I will let Fournier know to find you, thank you, Bill," said the Abbot, patting me on the shoulder as we parted ways.

Returning to the dorm, I asked my roommate if he had heard of this French Canadian seminarian. I had been so happy there, so "in my element", that it never occurred to me how hard it might be to settle into life in our solitary bluff community.

"Yeah, he's a shadow. Likes to sit in alcoves and write in his diary book."

"Diary book?"

"Smitty calls it the French book of Secrets."

"The Abbot asked me to tutor him in English so he might do better socializing."

"Well, well - an Abbot assignment. A rare ask... It won't take much to find him. He likes the alcoves in the tower the best. And apparently runs out in the forest in the morning. Hey, perhaps you've finally found a morning buddy. Albeit one that can't talk to you much."

"Perhaps I'll change that for him. Everyone deserves a chance to find their feet and their path here, eh?"

"Ah, that big farmboy heart of yours," Mitchell said, returning to his books for study.

As it turned out, Fournier found me first. I was in the small chapel at the piano, singing softly and chanting to the chords. The fall sun had just burst through the fog, bathing me and the piano in gems of reflective light from the ornate stained glass behind me.

"Ubi caritas et amor, Deus ibi est. Congregavit nos in unum Christi amor. Exultemus, et in ipso jucundemur. Timeamus, et amemus Deum vivum," I sang softly.

I ran my fingers over the Gregorian book before me, its square calligraphic notes, and the last of that verse. I hummed the melody, then softly sang the end of the chorus, "Et ex corde diligamus nos sincero."

And from a sincere heart let us love each other.

It was then I realized he was standing behind me, having silently entered the chapel while I was practicing.

I turned to speak to him, hesitating, losing my breath upon seeing the rough-faced man for the first time. He had one of those incalculable beards that seem to be dark and stubbly moments after the person shaves.

Friar Andreas would tell us that we wear the black cassock to remind a priest that he 'dies to the world' every day and immerses in eternity. Blackness also symbolizes giving up bright colors and thus giving up what the world brings, its glittering honors and entertainment. It made them merciless to keep clean, as stains were readily visible on black.

"It reminds the priest that he is held to a higher standard," Andreas would say. "His sins and failings will be more visible and judged more harshly than those of other people."

Milton Fournier stood in the chapel, his robes and cassock absolutely immaculate. Carved wooden rosary beads and a humble crucifix dangled from his belt. His dark features lit up with a colorful splash of stained glassed reflections.

We sat there for a delicious moment of warm silence.

"You are the one the others call…," he asked meekly, in a thick slurry of French accent, "eh, uh, 'ze Morning Monk?"

"Why yes, I suppose I am," I replied.

November 1977

Since I'd started tutoring Milton, the transformation was quick and quite amazing. He came out of his shyness and had become quite popular. His shyness gave way to reveal a generous man with a room-sized laugh, and a love of a soft-hearted prank on his classmates. They'd nicknamed him Mush after he had grown out his mustache and started waxing it into an old-fashioned curl.

He and I would trade off mornings at the gym and go out for runs in the woods. We would trade barbs about his classes, and constantly challenge him to learn new words.

We left for fall break, American students rushing home to our families for the Thanksgiving holiday. Mush had been asked along to spend the holiday with a family in Portland, and I caught my tiny flight home to the Palouse.

On our first meal together after the break, he went on and on about the amount of food Americans eat, and how his hosts treated him so nicely. I asked him if he missed his family back home in Quebec.

"I will see them at the long holiday. I do miss the crisp snow and the old world-ness of my home. Out here in the west - everything is so new, so young," he answered.

"But, your family?" I persisted.

"I suppose I do. My family is very, um, distant, even living close to one another. It is one, how you say, Frenchism that I have always disliked. My father is simply "in charge" but doesn't seem to have any opinions other than "you go study and become a priest." and Mother, she is proud of me, but lives in the shadow of my Father. I have an older brother, Guy. You would pronounce it Gee. He is the macho one. Football, your soccer. He is a hero at it. I am closer to my sister, Rachel. She and I share a softer view of the world. She escaped to college and doesn't come home often, but I'm sure she will for the Christmas.

Is it weird to say that what I miss most about Montreal is the fact that it is never completely quiet. There is always a car on the expressway, planes overhead and a bustle. It is after all, several cities in one. An old world capital trying to keep up with the latest age. I do miss home, though."

"Home for me is my family," I told him. "I am an only child and my parents are hippies turned farmers."

"Flower children?" Mush said with a wink.

"You have no idea. My mom would much rather see me become a college prof or something than be here. Pop and I trade letters and talk when we can. They both escaped a city like Montreal, and found each other farming out in the grasslands.

I didn't get the farming gene, it's all entirely too dirty and gross for me. And the slaughter, a necessary part of the cycle of farming, oh no. no. no," I said laughing. "Let's just say I hid animals once as a child so my Pop couldn't do it. It just wasn't meant to be.

So I'm here - learning how to lead a different kind of flock. As Peter says, 'Be shepherds of God's flock that is under your care, watching over them--not because you must, but because you are willing, as God wants you to be; not pursuing dishonest gain, but eager to serve.'"

"You seem to have a crush on St. Peter, William," Mush teased.

"I suppose I do. Peter is the patron saint of flaws. Of being imperfect but still realizing that God loves you anyhow. Peter can teach us how to deal with tough personalities like your father. We can be true to our family like our faith while accepting that our flaws are part of what make us human. It can make less of a struggle and more of a way to understand people who you don't always see eye to eye with."

"You do have such a compassionate view. That is an admirable thing, I think," he said with his soft smile.

I returned from class one morning to find an envelope addressed to me leaning against the standard issue lamp on my side table. I opened it up, reading for the first time his thick, luscious handwriting.

He began with 'Mon âme sceur' - as I fiddled with my French/English dictionary, I discovered it meant "my kindred spirit."

> *Mon* âme *sceur, Please accept my invitation to escape a bit this coming weekend. As much as scripture and study feeds our brain and pursuit of God, so should a nice hike and sharing nature and conversation out in the woods be beneficial for our hearts and minds. I noticed the painting in your room of the waterfall; so did a bit of looking to find us a waterfall to find together. To get to know what makes the morning monk come to where he is now. I hope to hear affirmatively soon. - Bests, Milton*

Silver Falls State Park

The following Saturday we met at breakfast in our civilian clothes. There was a particular freedom being away from our robes and formalities.

He pulled a bright red knit cap on as we walked to the bus stop. When he saw I'd only brought a baseball cap with me, he pulled out a second woolen knit cap.

"Mama makes these almost as fast as the tea cozies. She is constant with them. Here, try one."

Once on the bus he broke out a small leather journal and showed all the research he'd done on the falls, how it had started out like most foothill communities as a logging hub. How he thought we'd be the only people out there in the woods.

Glancing over his shoulder, I could see quotes and words to look up written in the margins and a hand-drawn map like something out of a Peter Pan story. A few pages had boxes labeled "Ask Morning" with words or topics written within them. His energy and excitement was contagious, and I listened intently.

With the bus ride soon behind us, we hiked deep in the woods, most of the time so quiet together, the crunch of the snow beneath our feet. It appeared we had the entire forest to ourselves. We hiked along and suddenly could start hearing the falls through the trees. I stopped, looking up into the filtered sunlight, rendering the browns, reds and stubborn greens like a stained glass window.

"Why are you here at St. Gertrude's?"

His voice softly broke the silence.

"Pardon?"

"Why are you here - at the seminary? What are you looking for?"

"To serve God - to help people find love."

"To find love. An interesting path," he said, "but..."

We walked a moment and I turned and replied, "but?"

"What about love for yourself?" he said.

He leaned in and softly kissed me. It took me so completely by surprise that I let the moment linger, letting him lean in against me before softly saying, "Oh Mush, this isn't a good idea."

Apparently, the stunned look on my face communicated a far more negative reaction.

"I am..... I am sorry...," he said, retreating.

"Oh my gosh. No. no" I said, reaching out to him, "Never be sorry for loving someone."

He stood there for a moment, framed by the trees and the snow looking so vulnerable and beautiful.

"But we are men of God. So that kind of love for ourselves is not our path."

"I know," he said meekly.

Mush stepped in behind me and gave a deliberate deep breath against my neck, wrapping his arms around me. I pulled his arms in against me in a strong hug.

"You are a special one, William."

We stood there in the woods wrapped up in each other for the longest time, then walked back down the trail to the bus stop.

"I hope," Milton said quietly, "that this doesn't change you, change us. I am worried."

"Oh Mush, of course not. One doesn't end being mon âme sceur because someone admits they love you. Loving each other and relying on our friendship will serve us well as we go off to our congregations. I think we'll be friends for many years, Mr. Fournier, you can count on it."

As the bus chugged down the road back towards the abbey, I took the opportunity to open Mush's journal to a new page and in my most artistic handwriting, I wrote John Muir's quote - "Another glorious day, the air as delicious to the lungs as nectar to the tongue."

December 1977

The notes became an almost daily ritual. He would ask me a question after morning prayer and I would answer it. What winter sports were closeby to attend? Why did I like Saint Paul so much? He started joining me on my predawn trips to the gym. Our notes started discussing art, my Rodin obsession, his love of Pollack and modern art. Almost imperceptibly, they became more and more personal. We learned our personal histories in this incredibly old-fashioned method.

November turned into the holiday season, and I soon found myself packing my things for Christmas break, when Mitchell, my roommate, handed me a taped note from Mush.

"He dropped this by while you were away" he said.

For a moment we kept packing, and then he spoke softly, "You need to be careful."

I tried to pretend that I hadn't heard him.

"Someone less....... understanding," he said, carefully choosing his words. "The notes, the little hikes together off in the woods. Someone less understanding might find something sinister in this."

"Sinister?" I said, reactively.

"If these letters were intercepted by the wrong people, just be careful, Bill. Mush is sweet on you and while it's adorable, mind where you are. You need to keep focused. The path from here must become more and more certain. Matters of love turning towards service and the church, and not the messy affairs of normal men," he said, paternally tapping me on the shoulder.

I tried to shake it off, remaining silent the entire cab ride to the airport.

Once aboard the plane, I unfolded the letter Milton had left for me in my room:

> *A merry and sacred holiday to you, mon* âme *sceur! It seems like I travel a world away from you to head back home to my family. The cobblestone streets of Montreal seem very far away.*

The Irish would burn the candles and keep the doors unlocked, that a Mary and Joseph, looking for a place to stay, would find their way to a home and be welcomed with open doors and open hearts. I am so thankful for how wondrously generous you have been to me at St. Gertrude's, and will light a candle in my window on Christmas Eve with an open heart, and think of you. Love, Mush.

Despite the warmth of his letter, my roommate's warning and appraisal rang in my head.

I broke out my journal and flipped through the hundreds of pages of daily entries about my sophomore fall at the Abbey. Bits of Latin in the margins. Bickering about profs and many mentions of Milton. My occasional French lessons from my friend made me smile as I flipped back through. Several bookmarks were my little notes to and from him.

As the journal flipped open to a clear page, I set the pen to work and almost involuntarily wrote, "Sinister."

New Year's Day - 1978

The phone rang on the line in something out of a black-and-white movie, making it sound a world away. The ringtone rang shorter. I tried to imagine what the house might look like on the other end.

"Hello," answered an abrupt female voice.

Glancing at the clock, I adjusted my greeting for the time change. "Good afternoon. Is Milton there, please?"

There was an odd pause before she answered, "No, he is not. Can I tell him who called?"

"Could you tell him, Bill from St. Gertrude's, please?" I told her, rattling off my phone number.

There was another long pause.

"You are Bill? The morning monk?"

Excited to hear my nickname, I replied, "Yes, ma'am, that is me."

"Forgive me my English, but...you shouldn't call here," she said softly, "His......engouement. His love. He has chosen a layperson's life. He is not returning to St. Gertrude's. It has caused a lot of heartache and misunderstanding, because him in the church was always the plan. To my parents, you are the sin. For them, you are blocking him from God. You...you can't call here. It will be bad for him."

"Is this Rachel? Will you tell him I called?" I said with a tone of disappointment.

"Yes. Yes, it is, but I will let him know, but... it is too explosif. Milt will find you. But you can't call here. Please."

There was a small pause before she fumbled the receiver and I heard the audible click of her hanging up.

February 3, 1978

I had returned to school from the Christmas holidays. Every morning I noticed Milton was gone.

I had spent my Christmas holiday wondering what it would be like to return to St. Gertrude's. The phone call I'd tried to surprise Milton with for a Christmas present told me all the things I needed to know before word came to me that the Abbot wished to see me. Being called to the Abbot's office is the spiritual equivalent of being asked to the principal's office.

"You've been a strong student here, top of all your classes. That is why you were asked to mentor underclassmen and to tutor some of them who were struggling. I returned from Christmas to receive a troubling letter from Milton Fournier resigning from school. What Mr. Fournier didn't know is that a letter came a few days later from his father. His family is having a crisis of faith since their son had chosen not to return to St. Gertrude's. That their son had decided he was gay after falling in love with a fellow student."

Setting the letter in front of me, he continued, "They say that they sent their son here to find God and to serve the church and he was presented with sin and behavior unsuitable for a man of the cloth. The letter calls you out by name, that Milton is in love with the 'morning monk.' This letter puts me in an awkward position, William. I am going to have to ask you some questions."

I sat wordlessly.

"Were you and Mr. Fournier in a sexual relationship?"

"No, Father. Just close friends," I said, tears starting up in my eyes. "Mush is my mon âme sœur."

The Abbot let out an audible sigh.

"Rules and structure are an important part of seminary life, you understand, Mr. Emory," began the Abbot, his switching to my formal last name not going unnoticed. *Non quam duo, semper tres.*"

"Not in twos, always threes," I translated involuntarily.

"You were placed in an esteemed position of leadership and scholarship."

"I did nothing wrong, Father. We are taught to love – to preach love. All I did was love Milton. Cannot two men love one another without it being viewed as sexual?"

"Mr. Fournier obviously thought it was romantic and homosexual. So much so that he turned his back on his faith and professed his love for you."

The two of us sat facing each other, silent, for what seemed like an eternity.

"The Seminary has no choice but to terminate its relationship with you, effective immediately. Since you are over 21, we did not notify your parents. You will be escorted to your room while your peers are in classes and taken to the bus station. As a courtesy, we will mail two boxes to your home address. You must be off the premises before evening prayer."

I sat silently.

"You are dismissed, Mr. Emory."

April 1978

I awoke from the dream sweating. A thick tangle of winter sheets and blankets restrained my feet, leaving my chest and arms exposed. The winds of February howled outside so that you could almost imagine they visibly struck the little house. The red digital clock on the nightstand announced 2:45am.

I relented, giving up on sleep, reaching to the pile of clothes on the floor, putting on a t-shirt and sweats. I quietly walked out to the kitchen and poured myself a glass of water. Another gust hit the house, making all the glasses and dishes in the open cupboard wince and shake. The streetlamp made shadows of the evergreens outside the kitchen window. As I set the glass down on the counter, the whirling dervish of shadows found their way up my arm and onto my chest.

How could I miss having someone in my bed next to me that I'd never had there in the first place? In the darkness, the thought of him filled my eyes with tears.

The clock in the hallway chimed, announcing it was 6am his time. He would have finished his prayers. Even in the crunchy snow of midwinter he would go out for a run. He'd find himself in a small cafe hovering over a steaming bowl of oats, with a freshly sacrificed square of butter. A small porcelain cup with espresso.

I smiled, imagining this unknowable morning routine.

Wiping tears away, I wandered my way back to bed. Remaking the sheets carefully, I pulled the blankets up. I reached over, as had become habit, and pulled the other pillow affectionately tight against my chest.

I missed him like nothing else. He seemed so far away.

"So, are you?" Pop had asked matter-of-factly one morning over coffee.

"I don't know, honestly," was my truthful reply. "I just don't know. I know that what I feel for Mush is more than just a normal friendship. But his family, his culture, he is so far away."

He leaned in and simply surrounded me in a safe, fatherly hug. "Give it time. It will figure itself out. My best advice, boy, is to be gentle on yourself."

Mom was acting like my exile from Saint Gertrude's was something to celebrate. She was full of ideas of what a young man with a B.A. in Business and almost a Masters in Divinity could do. My homecoming for her was a blessing.

"Damn repressive Catholic sexuality anyway. Not expressing physical love makes people miserable. Almost 30 years together and your father and I make love every day, sometimes twice," she offered in a spectacular overshare, making Pop blush a deep red.

"You are going to have questions. You are having to reevaluate everything. You are going to learn where your place is. But let's keep your mother from talking about our sex life at the breakfast table, shall we?"

We both laughed.

"The Abbot," he continued, "well, he was only doing his job, and Milton's father was only doing what he thought in his heart was the right thing to do. You can't be worryin' about what others are doin' when you have so much on your plate already. It's no use. Mom and me'll be here to support you whatever happens."

May 1978

There I sat surrounded by the packing boxes I'd hastily packed at St. Gertrude's. I was sorting books to donate back to the bookstore.

I was back in the room where I'd spent my childhood. The ones marked "Books and Bibles" remained tightly taped shut. I traced the words on the outside of the box, almost tearing up. I let out a loud, exasperated sigh when I realized my mom was watching me from the doorway.

"Oh my good boy, I am so sorry," she said.

"You only use those words when you are going to lecture me about something, and really, I'm not in the mood for it, okay?"

Rather than retreating, she took it as an entreaty and came and sat next to me on the floor.

"Do you think I was blind your entire childhood? Other boys were falling in love with Michelle and that Anna girl whose Pop owned the bowling alley. You? I can remember you staring lovelorn at Geoffrey and Robert at a very early age.

I wasn't sure what to do, honestly. You know your pop, he said to let it be. For a smart educated man, he can be such a hippy 'love-in' type sometimes. Those kind of live and let live, it'll all figure itself out platitudes don't really help."

"He means well," I replied. "I guess perhaps having a gay son is a bit of a burden. And one who was kicked out of seminary on top of it. I wonder if other people just think I'm broken. Oh gosh, I messed it all up."

"Did you though? Imagine how unhappy you'd have been if you'd stayed and never had an opportunity to find the love you really need. One thing we are sure of is that our son is NOT broken. You just tried a path, and it wasn't the right one. And for the record, you could never be a burden."

"God sure didn't turn out to be the love I thought he would be."

"Well, pronouns aside, the idea of God as all-encompassing makes it a bit hard to expect that he, she, or it would have time to love you in specifically the way you hoped. I know that expectations were high. But what about this Mush? This Milton you met, could he love you the way you want?"

"Oh Mom, he's remarkable," I said suddenly, and excited, before pausing and looking back at the boxes, but we never said 'let's be intimate' or 'let me love you.' We never had a chance to do so. We were inseparable and in love as much as you can be. He tried to tell me there was more all I could do was say 'we're at a seminary.'"

"Well, have you written him back? I mean - here we are in the green of springtime. Perhaps with this much distance between you and Gertrude's, you can concentrate on something good for a change?"

"No. I don't know how to answer him," I replied, glancing at his letter open on my dresser.

"Billy, perhaps telling him that you love him is a place to start? He took a great risk when he went home and told his family his real feelings. You never get what you don't ask for, right? How long has it been since his letter has sat there?" she asked, pointing to it.

"A couple of weeks. I don't know what to say to him. I do but I don't. I mean, he's just so far away."

"Honey, I don't know what is in that letter. It's your business. But what I do know? He's only as far away as you let him remain," she said, tussling my hair like she did when I was five. With that she left me alone in my room.

I picked up his letter, and re-read it.

Mon âme sœur....

Your idol Merton says, "The beginning of love is the will to let those we love be perfectly themselves, the resolution not to twist them to fit our own image. If in loving them we do not love what they are, but only their potential likeness to ourselves, then we do not love them: we only love the reflection of ourselves we find in them!"

So - it is important to say - I am unsure whether my love for you was felt in the same way - and I may have done you a grave injustice and harm by proclaiming so in a time of stress and angst.

Oh what a mess of things. So much has transpired. I will do my best to tell you why it has been so long for you to to hear from me. I was selfish at the holidays. I had fallen in love with you, while sleeping nights in a seminary. My timing was not the best for me to discover it. I returned home for the holidays - and told my sister about you, how we met. That beautiful day in the small chapel.

Anyways - my mother overheard the conversation. Things very quickly escalated from there, my special friend, as you can imagine. My father does not understand the modern world, and reacted poorly. I was eventually was packed

Mon âme sœur....

Your idol Merton says, "The beginning of love is the will to let those we love be perfectly themselves, the resolution not to twist them to fit our own image. If in loving them we do not love what they are, but only their potential likeness to ourselves, then we do not love them: we only love the reflection of ourselves we find in them."

So – it is important to say – I am unsure whether My love for you was felt in the same way – and I may have done you a grave injustice and harm by proclaiming so in a time of stress and angst.

Oh what a mess I have made of things. So much has transpired. I will do my best to tell you why it has been so long for you to hear from me. I was selfish at the holidays. I had fallen in love with you; while sleeping nights in a seminary. My timing was not the best for me to discover it. I returned home for the holidays – and told my sister about you, how we met. That beautiful day in the small chapel.

Anyways – my mother overheard the conversation. Things very quickly escalated from there, my special friend, as you can imagine. My father does not understand the modern world, and reacted poorly. I eventually was packed and out living with my older brother. The tension it caused my family to be honest was nothing to how the news must have affected you when it reached you. I received a letter from John at Gertrude's about your sudden departure.

It gave me such a heartache to know that my choice to change paths, had undone yours as well.

I daydream of us.

My brain untwists itself and lays flat. I think to myself, but god how much I want you to touch me. How long can a person live without physical affection? How are people supposed to live like this? I want to wake realizing that you are touching that rise at the base of my neck, perhaps feel your breath shortly afterwards, rendering from deep within me a soft whimper of please do that again. How do I dream of such things we have yet to know about one another?

I write you from a coffee shop on St. Catherine. Catherine is an interesting story — martyred by the Romans for being eloquent and educated. Curious that our saint, Harvey Milk, suffered the same fate. It pleases me that while no *and out and living with my older brother. The tension it caused my family for me to be honest was nothing to how the news must have affected you when it reached you. I received a letter from John at Gertrude's about your sudden departure.*

It gave me such heartache to know that my choice to change paths, had undone yours as well.

I daydream of us,

my brain untwists itself and lays me flat. I think to myself, but god how much I want you to touch me. How long can a person live without physical affection? How are people supposed to live like this? I want to wake realizing that you are touching that rise at the base of my neck. Perhaps feel your breath there shortly afterwards, rendering from deep within me a soft whimper of please do that agains. How do I dream of such things we have yet to know about one another?

I write you from a coffee shop on Saint Catherine. Catherine is an interesting story – martyred by the Romans for being eloquent and educated. Curious that our saint, Harvey Milk, suffered the same fate. It pleases me that while no longer a novice heading for priesthood, my faith and its history still present comfort.

You'd laugh — as I am tutoring students on my work. I'm lating aid in the basics of English. Also a few mathematics students

I ~~still~~ need to get this in the post.... but William, my dear friend, I hope I can hear back from you, and we can discuss ourselves, and that you can forgive me for what I have done. You ~~will~~ always said that truth is important. The truth is that I love you and am glad I have met you.

— Yours — Mosh

P.S. — Faith is confidence about things hoped for and conviction about things unseen. (Hebrews 11:1)

longer a novice heading for priesthood my faith and its history still presents comfort.

You'd laugh – as I am tutoring students as my work. In Latin and in the basics of English. Also a few mathematics students.

I need to get this in the morning post... but William. my dear friend. I hope I can hear back from you, and we can discuss ourselves, and that you can forgive me for what I have done. You always said that truth is important. The truth is that I love you and am glad I have met you.

– Yours – Mush

P.S. - Faith is confidence about things hoped for and conviction about things unseen. (Hebrews 11:1)

Dearest Mush

I was delighted to receive your letter.

I am so very sorry it took me so long to write you back.

Let me begin with this: I Love You, Milton Fournier—and have from the moment I saw you in the small chapel. I still start each day with my morning prayers. I thank God, then I thank him for you.

I always say it with your accent, Meh-l-Ton. It rolls from my tongue like a poem of hope. It makes your name my morning prayer. I know that our meeting was a moment of grace.

Reading your handwriting again after so long makes me very emotional. Oh, I have missed you. It took me a little while to think what to say to you.

I have included a photograph inside

Dearest Mush,

I was delighted to receive your letter.

I am so very sorry it took me so long to write you back.

Let me begin with this: I Love You, Milton Fournier - and have from the moment I saw you in the small chapel. I still start each day with my morning prayers. I thank God, then I thank Him for you.

I always say it with your accent, Meh-I-Ton. It rolls from my tongue like a poem of hope. It makes your name my morning prayer. I know that our meeting was a moment of grace.

Reading your handwriting again after so long makes me very emotional. Oh, I have missed you. It took me a little while to think what to say to you.

I have included a photograph inside

here for you to see. It is of the three of us. Meet my mother and father, Philip and Margaret.

I do see you so clearly in your coffee shop in Montreal. I see YOU clearly. St. Paul is the first to tell us that love can never be selfish - that it is patient and kind.

I got a big chuckle out of you using Merton to make your point. How you struggled through his writings! He can be dense for someone that has lived speaking English, leave alone a Frenchie like yourself.

Coming home from Saint Gertrude's was a somewhat less political landing for me. My parents are children of the sixties with far less attachment to firm ideas on just about any subject. My mother *here for you to see. It is of the three of us. Meet my mother and father, Philip and Margaret.*

I do see you so clearly in your coffee shop in Montreal. I see YOU clearly. St. Paul is the first to tell us that love can never be selfish – that it is patient and kind.

I got a big chuckle out of you using Merton to make your point. How you struggled through his writings! He can be dense for someone that has lived speaking English, leave alone a Frenchie like yourself.

Coming home from Saint Gertrude's was a somewhat less political landing for me. My parents are children of the sixties with far less attachment to firm ideas on just about any subject. My mother was relieved, and actually admitted she had been deeply conflicted about me and the church. My father, well, he is a philosopher and thinker, much like you. He preached gentleness. You would love my father. Your hearts are both on your sleeves.

Spring is happening here in the Palouse, the rolling grasses are turning every shade of green imaginable! The seasons of change have always been my favourite, the falls and the springs. I am actually working part time at a bakery in our town here. It is not lost on me that Trappists bake bread, and I am now learning that trade as well. I am saving up to be able to come see you. I think. I think seeing you is important, and if this between us is what we think it is, finding a safe *was relieved, and actually admitted she had been deeply conflicted about me and the church. My father, well, he is a philosopher and thinker, much like you. He preached gentleness. You would love my father. Your hearts are both on your sleeves.*

Spring is happening here in the Palouse, the rolling grasses are turning every shade of green imaginable. The seasons of change have always been my favourite, the falls and the springs.

I am actually working part time at a bakery in our town here. It is not lost on me that Trappists bake bread, and I am now learning that trade as well. I am saving up to be able to come see you. I think. I think seeing you is important. And if this between us is what we think it is, finding a safe place where we might experience a sunrise together?

Probably far away from your Pop.

I am more sure every day that the love you were brave enough to call out – is reflected here in my heart. When years have passed – we will think of St. Gertrude's less; and having found each other more.

– Not even my mother calls me William

Love, Your William.

place where we might experience a sunrise together.

Probably far away from your Pop.

I am more sure every day that the love you were brave enough to call out – is reflected here in my heart. When years have passed – we will think of St. Gertrude's less; and having found each other more.

- Not even my mother calls me William -

Love, Your William.

My William,

Thank you, my love for your words and
your prayers. I did not have good
patience waiting for your reply and now
that I have heard from you, I keep your
photo with me always. It is under
my pillow at night, and in my satchel
with me during the day.

Your parents are darling. Philip! Margarett!
       I send my love.

Your notion that loving me becomes your
morning prayer makes me so happy.
I knew that if you did indeed feel that way
you'd know the perfect way to express it.
It is crazy crazy that it's only been four
months since we walked near the falls.
It makes feels like an eternity for so many
reasons.

My father continues to give me the silent
treatment, and judge my brother for taking
me in. I owe Guy so very much. Once I
find a job, though, I will be out on my own
soon.

My William,

Thank you my love for your words and your prayers. I did not have good patience waiting for your reply and now that I have heard from you, I keep your photo with me always. It is under my pillow at night, and in my satchel with me during the day.

Your parents are darling. Philip! Margaret! I send my love.

Your notion that loving me becomes your morning prayer makes me so happy. I knew that if you did indeed feel that way you'd know the perfect way to express it.

It is crazy that it's only been four months since we walked near the falls. It feels like an eternity for so many reasons.

My father continues to give me the silent treatment, and judge my brother for taking me in. I owe Guy so very much. Once I find a job, though, I will be out on my own soon.

It is an uncomfortable thing being so alone when you don't want to be

I spend time daydreaming about your Idaho, your grassy Palouse. I wonder what it is like to live in such a rural place. I found a guidebook at the bookstore, and I am reading it about places we can go hiking and camping. Thinking of our adventuring together makes the cold of winter and the struggle to get out on my own easier to bear...

Please find enclosed a hiking guide to Quebec. So that we might dream of adventures, I have dog eared the pages of hikes that I think you'd like the most. Along with a bookmark......

Moshi

It is an uncomfortable thing being so alone when you don't want to be.

I spend time daydreaming about your Idaho, your grassy Palouse. I wonder what it is like to live in such a rural place. I found a guidebook at the bookstore, and I am reading about places we can go hiking and camping. Thinking of our adventuring together makes the cold of winter and the struggle to get out on my own easier to bear.

Please find enclosed a hiking guide to Quebec. So that we might dream of adventures, I have dog eared the pages of hikes that I think you'd like the most. Along with a bookmark......

June 1978

I got home from the bakery and found the house surprisingly quiet.

"Hey, Pop. Where's Mom?"

"At her PFLAG meeting."

"Her what meeting?"

"PFLAG - Parents and Friends of Lesbians and Gays."

"Really?" I said with a chuckle.

"It shouldn't surprise you that your mother started it. When you came home, you know your mother. She never got the whole Catholic thing, and well, when we learned why you'd come home, it was like she'd been given a project. She was worried what people would say at the grocery store or if people would talk about you in a bad way. And her attitude was clearly 'not about my son they won't' - followed by some kind of truck stop cursing. Again, you know your mother, you can take the girl off the farm, but the farm stays. So she went and checked out some books at the library."

While my Dad continued speaking I imagined my headstrong mother showing up at our small Idaho town library. "My son is a fag and I need to read up about what that means."

"She brought home a book that read like a pet owner's manual. The title was literally something like 'So your son is gay.' And that led her to finding out about PFLAG. Talk about a match made in heaven – it's sort of an interesting mix of Tupperware parties and talking about gay kids. Which is why you see me here at home reading instead of joining her."

"Where are the meetings?"

"She's holding them at the library in the conference room. Of the parents, she is the only parent of a gay son, and everyone else that has started showing up have lesbian daughters. Apparently, the Palouse is a hotbed for young lesbians. Who knew?"

"This is all pretty amazing and crazy and unexpected, you know that?"

"Well, we figured we had two choices. Go on the journey with you, and it'll all get figured out, or let you fumble around in the dark without any help. And who does that benefit? Nobody. Right?"

July 1978

The beauty was in the simplicity of it:

> *Together with their families, Kimberley Brockman and Loren Steiner invite you*
> *to celebrate their marriage! Sunday, 15 July, 1978 at two o'clock in the afternoon*

As a family we dressed in our best, Mom beamed in her bright sundress, Dad and I in suits. I wasn't exactly on speaking terms with God, I was honestly pretty pissed off with him. I'd spent the springtime in this quiet brooding mood. There I was, suddenly at the wedding of a high school friend and her new husband. We shuffled into the local parish and it wasn't lost on any of us this was my first time back since I had returned from St. Gertrude's that winter.

Kimberley and I had been in theater shows together as teenagers, and she'd brought Loren around during her first year in college and they were quickly engaged. They'd come home to her childhood church to get married.

It was picture perfect, that fairy tale hush that came over the crowd as the door opened and her father walked her down the aisle. The liturgy and exchange of vows, and then she pulled back her veil and shared a beautiful kiss with her new husband.

They walked down the aisle, Mr. and Mrs. She winked at me on the way by and mouthed, "Thank you for coming!" I joined my parents at the reception, watching everyone go through this ageless ritual. I caught myself thinking to myself what a wonderful time Mush would have had at such a gathering. His laughter could light up a room. He had a laugh like a small child, the kind that just makes everyone else around him smile. My parents and I made a short time of it and headed back home. I was surprised by a phone call from Kimberley - apologizing that we'd not gotten to spend a lot of time together, and that we should do lunch before they left town.

"That Kimberley doesn't miss much," Mom said as I set the phone down. "Her mother was asking me all kinds of questions, what you were going to do next, and I told her that it'd be best if Kimberley asked you herself."

"Was Mrs. Brockman gossiping about me?", I said.

"No, dear. Believe it or not - there are people in this world that love you besides your Dad and me. Go have lunch with the girl. Besides, she's a married woman now, she won't bite ya."

I got off work at the bakery and headed across the town square to the diner. The place was thick with memories. Coming in there after a theater show in high school and they set a giant overflowing plate of french fries and bottomless rootbeers down and we'd test the boundaries of "open late" on the staff every time. Catching me lost in thought, Kimberley was suddenly sitting next to me.

"Whatchya' thinking about, Mister?"

I smiled, "Well, hello, Mrs. Steiner!"

"Seriously, you were just staring off thinking. what's up? It doesn't seem like a party face you have going on."

"I was just thinking about all of us around the table over there trying to out-Monty-Python each other."

"That's what people are like when they are with someone they love. Ya know, I haven't been around town, but I keep my tabs on people. I can't imagine returning here has been easy for you."

"Yeah- well I'm working at the bakery till I can figure out what's next."

"What is next for a former seminarian? Please promise me you aren't going...... Episcopalian," she said with an overly dramatic fake gasp.

"Nah, I think God is still on a time out. And I think eventually, I'll move to the city. When I first got back from school, I struggled really hard with how bad it looked, how it had all ended. I know that anger and love are not mutually exclusive things. But I didn't know how to separate out what is God and what is my religion. And even within my religion, I don't know how to save what is good, and let go of the stuff that is harmful."

"Lots easier to be gay there I suppose than small town Idaho," she replied matter-of-factly.

I shot her a look of surprise.

"Oh, Billy, please. You were everyone's favorite gay kid in school, and well, so many priests are gay I just figured that was going to be your thing. So - San Francisco?"

"I'm thinking more eastward...."

"What's his name?" she said, realizing why. There never was keeping anything from her.

"Milton. Our friendship or rather us," I said using airqoutes,"was why we both ended up leaving St. Gert's."

"Oh, how romantic! So, what do you think God thinks of all this?"

"Oh, him? Believe me, when it started to occur to me, I thought 'well, I'll just pray about it.' I couldn't even honestly try to "pray away the gay." The words would stick in my throat; I didn't want it to go away. This was love. It was one of the purest, most beautiful things I'd ever felt. It felt like an insult to God to pretend that I thought it was anything other than a gift. So I'm just putting in my time at the bakery till I can save up and go find him."

"Feel your way into the truths of what you're going through! There's no rush. If you're angry with God, be angry with God. I think it's safe to say that she will understand. If you are angry with God, think how angry God must be with the people who made you feel that way. You asked how you can let go of the bad and hold on to the good? I don't think that's a concern. Because I think that, as it always has, the good is holding onto you. And that means the bad, all on its own, will continue to fall away from you.

If anyone deserves a good old-fashioned love affair, it's you, my friend! It's almost the 1980s, you need to just go be who you are. Good old straight as an arrow Idaho, "she said, motioning around her, "will survive without you. Perhaps it's won't twinkle quite as much, but the thought of loving someone and not just jumping in the deep end... Promise me you will as soon as you can?"

October 3, 1978

He and I saw each other again in person on a humid fall afternoon on a cobblestone alleyway in Montreal. His dark beard in full, wearing a bright red tank top and plaid shorts. Barefoot, as he has always preferred. I had flown the red eye, my hair a tumbled mess, and a weariness in my eyes that was palpable.

I had packed a backpack with my Bible, a brand new passport, my journal, and a camera. I'd tearfully said goodbye to my mom and dad. I literally showed up on the street in Montreal with nothing.

He saw me walking up the street and burst into tears. I dropped my bag and purposefully wiped his eyes with the handkerchief from my pocket. As if we'd been doing it our entire lives, we kissed and embraced there on the street until we could no longer stand.

He growled French words into my ear and then finally smiled and asked if I'd like to come inside. Nearly 30 years later, it is still our home.

Our entire lives are informed by that first year meeting at St. Gertrude's. Every Sunday he comes by the bakery we own - - every morning "The Morning Monk" light snaps on and we greet St. Catherine with strong coffee and pastries. Our regulars always smile, wave, and greet me with "Morning, Monsieur Monk!"

Mush will arrive quietly as we're cleaning up from the post-church crowd. He'll sit at the corner table, reading patiently, in his finest suit accessorized with some ridiculously cheery bowtie.

I'll finally give up and toss the key at the manager so that Mush and I can take our walk through parks and streets of our city. We take our weekly stroll, our 'hand holdy walk' as he calls it, taking the time to share the day together, rain or shine. Our life has become a string of rituals like this that neither of us will miss for the world.

"Oh, before I forget," Mush will say, the same joke every week. "God was in a really great mood this morning, she says hello by the way, and that you could take a Sunday off and join me sometime."

"God is great at a polite distance," I will, say winking back.

Now in our fortieth year together, we are one of those couples everyone knows. The French have a term for couples like us, *Piliers De La Maison*, the pillars of the house. A relationship on such a strong foundation, it holds the rest of the community up.

Mush is now a professor, teaching religious studies at Concordia. I imagine him arguing Merton or the crusades or the life of St. Peter in the halls. He still reads and studies feverishly, like he did at seminary.

He still draws in his diary, leaving little notes about people he observes. He has even entered some of his drawings in shows, and will occasionally teach a "walking and drawing" class at the community center. His world view remains soft and gentle, as always.

We spoil his sister's kids and grandkids. They call us a single blurred name when we show up, "Miltn'Monk." Mush's brother Guy and I are in a football league together.

My folks adore him, as they knew they would. Mush and Pop still insist on trading letters the "old world" way. Mush tries to "out share" my mother at the dinner table when they visit. With email these days and video calls, they feel closer than ever.

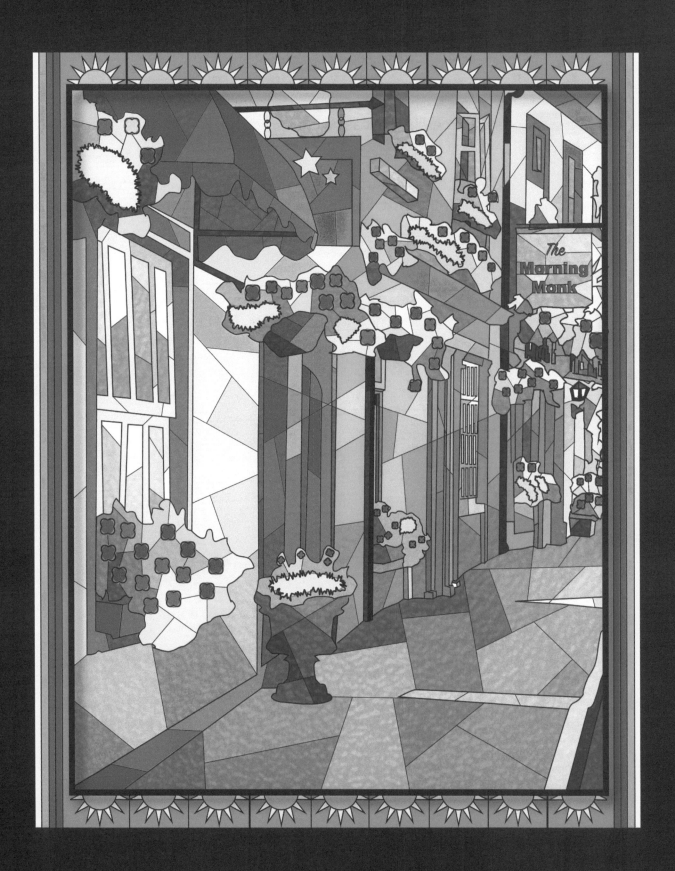

Every evening as the day winds down, we unplug from the world. While I pour a matching pair of scotches, Mush prepares a hot bubble bath. It always feels like such an extravagance to end our days like this, bathing together. We'll head to bed cuddled like velcro, my scruffy beard fitting perfectly into the corner of his neck.

It is the most natural, beautiful thing I can imagine. His gentle, honest whimpers of pleasure when in my arms reminds me what a blessing it is every day. My Mush stills takes my breath away whenever he walks in the room.

We each wear a puzzle piece around our necks carved from wood. A simple two-piece puzzle which we are both sure was true from the moment we saw one another. Each with a simple Latin phrase inscribed on the back,

"*Et ex corde diligamus nos sincero.*"

"And from a sincere heart let us love each other."

Milton

and the

Morning Monk

Author Biography

As a self-described disciple of Henry David Thoreau, Robert McDiarmid is both a writer and an activist. He works very hard to live an uncomplicated life in complicated times.

Robert resides in Palo Alto, CA with his husband David. An avid cyclist, he has participated several years in AIDS Lifecycle, a 550-mile bicycle ride from San Francisco to Los Angeles and the Friends for Life Bike Rally from Toronto to Montreal, Canada. In the spirit of giving back to the community, the entirety of his royalties are donated back to HIV/AIDS charities.

Robert's other works include his first novel is"*The House of Wolves*" from Lethe Press, "*Brief Moments*" *- a collection of short stories*" from CreateSpace, as well as a contributor to the romance anthology "*A Taste of Honey*" from Dreamspinner Press with his short story "*The Do-It-Yourself Guide to Getting Over Yourself.*"

CPSIA information can be obtained
at www.ICGtesting.com
Printed in the USA
LVHW070824060922
727658LV00002B/14